Stolen
Author
Read
Point Value: 1.0
ACCELERATED READER QUIZ 123141
Lexile Value: 540L

W9-ASV-686

Property Of
Title I
Renfroe Middle School
City Schools of Decatur

STOLEN BASES

BY JAKE MADDOX

illustrated by Tuesday Mourning

text by Val Priebe

Librarian Reviewer
Chris Kreie
Media Specialist, Eden Prairie Schools, MN
MS in Information Media, St. Cloud State University, MN

Reading Consultant
Mary Evenson
Middle School Teacher, Edina Public Schools, MN
MA in Education, University of Minnesota

STONE ARCH BOOKS

Impact Books are published by Stone Arch Books,
A Capstone Imprint
151 Good Counsel Drive, P.O. Box 669
Mankato, Minnesota 56002
www.capstonepub.com

Copyright © 2009 by Stone Arch Books

All rights reserved. No part of this publication may be reproduced
in whole or in part, or stored in a retrieval system, or transmitted in any
form or by any means, electronic, mechanical, photocopying, recording,
or otherwise, without written permission of the publisher.

Library of Congress Cataloging-in-Publication Data
Maddox, Jake.
  Stolen Bases / Jake Maddox; illustrated by Tuesday Mourning.
  p. cm. — (Impact Books. A Jake Maddox Sports Story)
  ISBN 978-1-4342-0779-1 (library binding)
  ISBN 978-1-4342-0875-0 (pbk.)
  [1. Softball—Fiction.] I. Mourning, Tuesday, ill. II. Title.
PZ7.M25643Stl 2009
[Fic]—dc22   2008004297

Summary: Someone is stealing the equipment from Eva and Becca's
softball team.

Art Director: Heather Kindseth
Graphic Designer: Kay Fraser

Printed in the United States of America in Stevens Point, Wisconsin.
012010
005661R

TABLE OF CONTENTS

CHAPTER 1
THE SAME OLD CREW

Becca rode her bike as fast as she could along the side streets, making sure to watch for cars. It was a warm June evening. The sun wouldn't set for hours, and Becca was on her way to the first softball practice of the summer.

Becca played in the local summer softball league. She had been looking forward to starting practice since school let out a couple of weeks earlier.

Soon, Becca arrived at the softball field. Her best friend, Eva, was already standing on the field with a bunch of other girls and their coach.

Becca recognized all of the other players. It looked like the team would be the same as it had been the year before.

Too bad, Becca thought. She had been hoping to see some new faces this year.

As Becca parked and locked up her bike, Eva spotted her and ran over.

"Hey!" said Eva. "It's the same old crew on the Lions this summer. We have Coach Jones again, too."

"I saw her," said Becca. "I wish there were some new girls, though," she added. "It would be really fun to meet some new people."

Just then, Coach Jones blew her whistle. Becca and Eva headed over with the rest of the team. All ten girls gathered around their coach.

"Hi, girls!" the coach said, smiling. "It's nice to see you all again. I hope you're having good summer vacations so far." All the players clapped.

Coach continued, "Our first game is scheduled for Saturday. We don't have much time, so let's get to work. Give me four laps around the bases and then head out to the outfield for stretches."

Becca and Eva jogged around the diamond together. After they'd finished four laps, they headed to the outfield. Once everyone was done running, Coach Jones led the team in stretches.

When they were finished, Coach Jones said, "Okay, everyone. Find a partner, grab your gloves and a ball, and spread out in the field. We're going to warm up a little before we get into some hitting drills."

Eva and Becca didn't need to talk about it. They were always partners. Together, they jogged to the dugout and grabbed their gloves.

Becca dug a softball out of the tall canvas bag where Coach Jones stored them. Then the girls headed out to right field and started to toss the ball back and forth.

Becca and Eva had been friends for eight years, since kindergarten. They'd been playing softball together almost as long. As they tossed the ball back and forth, it was clear that they loved playing together.

Becca was tall and quick. She could throw hard and fast, so she played shortstop.

Eva was shorter and had very strong arms. That was perfect for playing catcher, which required her to throw from her knees.

Eva sighed happily. "I love softball season," she said, picking the ball out of her glove and throwing it easily back to Becca. "Don't you?"

Becca laughed. "You know it!" she said, smiling. Then she frowned. "Hey, who's that over by the left field fence?" she asked.

Eva turned and squinted against the setting sun. A girl was standing alone outside the fence. "That blond girl all by herself?" Eva asked.

"Yeah," replied Becca. "Do you recognize her?"

"No," Eva said. "I've never seen her before in my life."

Then Coach Jones blew her whistle. Becca and Eva forgot all about the unfamiliar girl.

CHAPTER 2
STOLEN
EQUIPMENT

After warm-ups on the second day
of practice, all the girls crowded around
Coach Jones at home plate.

"All right, everyone," the coach said.
"Make sure you're all stretched out, and I'll
go get the equipment bag."

Becca sat down next to Eva and
stretched her legs out. She carefully bent
over, reaching her hands toward her feet.
The stretch felt great.

Suddenly, she heard Coach Jones yell from the storage shed.

As quickly as she could, Becca got up and ran over to the shed. She pulled the door open.

Coach was standing inside. She had her hands on her hips and an angry look on her face.

"What's wrong, Coach? Are you okay?" asked Becca, worried.

Coach Jones crossed her arms and shook her head. "The equipment bag is missing," she said. "Who would take a bag full of balls and bats?" She sighed angrily.

"Wow!" Becca said. "That really stinks."

"Yes, it does," Coach Jones replied. "Well, I guess practice is over. I don't have any other equipment."

They walked out of the shed. Most of the team was gathered outside. "What's the matter?" asked one of the girls.

"The equipment bag is missing," said Coach Jones. "We're going to have to cancel practice today."

Everyone started talking at once. Coach Jones raised a hand to quiet them. She said, "We don't have any equipment. We don't have anything to practice with. I'm really sorry, girls."

"I have an idea, Coach," Eva said. "My house is right across the street. We have bats and a couple of softballs. Do you want me to go get them?"

"Why didn't I think of that?" said Becca, pretending to smack herself on the forehead.

"Eva, you're a lifesaver!" exclaimed Coach. "Go get them!"

"I'll come with you," said Becca.

The two girls ran as fast as they could to Eva's house. In the garage, they found three softballs. Then Eva grabbed a couple of bats and they ran back to the field.

When they reached the team, everyone was still trying to figure out what had happened to their equipment. All of the girls were talking about it.

"Girls, we're not going to figure it out tonight," said Coach. "Let's get down to business. Eva, you catch. Sasha and Ashley can take turns pitching. Laura, Becca, and Maria, you three spread out in the outfield. Not too far, though. The rest of you are going to take turns hitting."

Becca and the two other outfielders jogged out to the grass. The two pitchers started warming up their throwing arms.

Eva grabbed her shin guards, which, luckily, she'd kept at home, instead of with the other equipment. Coach Jones helped her put her shin guards on. The girls who were waiting to hit warmed up by stretching their shoulders.

Finally, they were ready to start practicing. The first girl up to bat hit a line drive down the third base line. In the outfield, Becca hurried to grab the ball. She threw it back to the pitcher.

With a loud clang, the second girl at bat popped the ball straight up in the air. Eva had to throw off her mask to look up and catch the ball.

After a while, the girls in the outfield traded places with three of the hitters. When it was Becca's turn to bat, she swung as hard as she could and hit the ball over the left field fence.

She easily made it around all the bases. But as one of the fielders ran to get the ball, Becca noticed something strange.

That same blond girl from the day before was back, watching them from behind the right field fence.

CHAPTER 3
SOMETHING'S WEIRD

The next day after lunch, Becca rode her bike over to Eva's house. They sat on Eva's porch, drinking homemade strawberry lemonade.

"So where do you think it went?" asked Eva, her eyes closed to keep out the bright afternoon sun.

"The equipment bag?" Becca asked. "Well, I'm pretty sure it didn't walk off on its own!"

Eva rolled her eyes and laughed. "I know that it didn't walk off on its own," she said, looking over at Becca. "But who would take it?"

"I don't know," replied Becca. "It's kind of weird. I mean, there's a whole bunch of other stuff in the storage shed. I saw it yesterday. Footballs and soccer balls and stuff. Why would they take the softball equipment but nothing else?"

"Maybe Coach Jones just left it at her house and forgot about it," said Eva.

"Yeah, maybe," said Becca. But Eva could tell she didn't really think so.

* * *

After dinner, the girls grabbed their gloves. They walked across the street to the field for practice.

As they rounded the corner of the shed, they found Coach Jones. She was looking through the equipment bag.

"Hey, the bag is here!" Eva said.

"Yes," Coach Jones said slowly.

"Where did you find it?" Becca asked.

"It's the funniest thing," Coach Jones replied. "I went to the store last night and bought more equipment. More balls and bats and even a few mitts. I got here this afternoon and was getting ready to store the new equipment. And that's when I found our bag!"

Eva and Becca looked at each other.

"This is so weird," Becca said. "Why would someone take the bag from the shed one day and then bring it back the very next day?"

"And who would do that?" asked Eva. "I mean, borrowing the equipment bag? It doesn't make any sense."

"No, it really doesn't," said Coach Jones. She thought for a minute. Then she went on, "Well, I'm just glad it's back. Ready for practice?"

"Yeah," said Eva.

Becca wasn't listening. Something else had caught her eye. The same blond girl was standing behind the right field fence again.

CHAPTER 4
BORROWED?

After practice, Becca went back to Eva's house. As they watched TV in Eva's living room, Becca couldn't stop thinking about the girl she'd seen hanging around the softball field.

Becca said, "Most criminals return to the scene of the crime, right?"

Eva laughed. "What are you talking about?" she asked. "Have you been watching detective shows or something?"

Becca shook her head. "No. I'm just thinking about the equipment bag," she explained. "I think whoever borrowed it will probably go back and borrow it again."

"Borrowed?" Eva asked. "Don't you mean stole?"

Becca frowned. "I don't think so," she said. "No one who was really stealing something would bring back the thing that they stole."

"That's true," Eva said thoughtfully.

"Anyway," Becca said, "I think we should stay up and catch whoever was borrowing the bag. If they come back tonight, we can figure out who it was. And maybe we can stop them."

Eva thought about it for a while. Finally, she nodded.

"Okay," Eva said. "I see what you're saying. I'll get Mark to set up the tent in the front yard. We can see the field really well from there."

While Eva's older brother, Mark, set up the family tent in the front yard, Eva and Becca gathered their supplies. They made several trips between the house and the tent with sleeping bags, pillows, flashlights, and snacks.

By the time they crawled into the tent, it was dark out. The night air quickly turned cool. Eva made one more trip to the house to find two sweatshirts that they could wear.

Finally, she crawled into the tent. "So what are we going to do if we catch the thief?" asked Eva. She opened a bag of chips and popped a few into her mouth.

"I don't know," replied Becca. She took a long drink of soda. "I guess we could call the police. Or we could ask the person to turn themselves in."

"I just don't understand why someone would do this," said Eva.

"Yeah, I know," said Becca, shaking her head. "We probably won't understand until we find out who did it." She let out a long breath. Then she asked, "Can we talk about something else?"

"Like what?" asked Eva.

"How about . . ." said Becca, pausing to turn her flashlight on Eva. "Boys!" she said in a silly voice.

Squinting in the beam of the flashlight, Eva blushed bright red. They both started giggling and didn't stop for a long time.

The girls stayed awake as long as they could, but they didn't see anyone near the softball field.

Neither girl knew what time it was, but the neighborhood was quiet when they both started drifting off to sleep. The excitement of the day had tired them both out.

The last thing Becca said before closing her eyes was, "I really hope our bag is there tomorrow."

CHAPTER 5
500!

The next day at practice, everything was back to normal. No one had forgotten about the strange things happening to the bag, but everyone was excited for their game against Springfield on Saturday. It was only two days away.

After the players warmed up with laps and stretches, Coach Jones said, "Everyone grab your gloves and spread out in the field! We're going to play 500!"

All the girls cheered. 500 was a really fun game to play. Plus, Coach Jones usually gave a prize to the winner.

"I'll hit," Coach Jones said. "I'll use a t-ball stand so no one will have to pitch or catch."

The rules of 500 were pretty simple. As Coach Jones hit each ball, she would call out a number.

Whoever caught the ball won that round, and would get as many points as the number Coach called out. Whoever got to 500 points first would be the winner of the game.

Becca knew she had to be careful, though. Coach was famous for yelling out negative numbers that would make a score go down!

"Make sure you're listening when I yell out the points," Coach Jones said. "Okay, let's play!"

The softball players ran to the field. They all spread out.

"The rules are the same as last year," Coach Jones shouted. "Everyone keep track of your own score. First girl to get 500 points wins a prize." She placed a t-ball stand at home plate and set a ball on top.

The girls were all in position. "Everybody ready?" yelled Coach. Then she gripped the bat and swung.

The ball flew to the outfield as Coach shouted, "Fifty points!"

"Mine!" Eva called. She put her glove up to catch the ball. With a muffled thunk, the ball landed in her glove.

"Nice catch, Eva," Becca said.

Eva grinned. "Thanks!" she said, throwing the ball back to Coach.

Coach Jones swung and hit the ball again. "Two hundred!" she yelled.

"Got it!" called Becca. She caught the ball with a smile and threw it back to Coach.

The game took up the rest of that day's practice. Becca and Eva and their teammates ran all over the field, catching balls and sending them back to Coach Jones.

Every once in a while, Coach would yell out a negative number, just to make sure they were paying attention. Once, Eva stopped herself just in time to let a negative ball hit the ground.

The game finally ended when Coach hit a high ball that flew way into the outfield. She yelled "Five hundred!"

Since Becca was taller and faster than almost everyone else, she ran back and caught it.

"Yay!" she yelled. She'd never won 500 before. It felt great!

"Way to go, Becca!" Eva said, smiling.

"Nice job, everyone," said Coach. She pulled something out of her pocket and held it out toward Becca. "Here's your prize, Becca. You did a great job today."

Becca smiled. "Thanks, Coach," she said. She opened the small envelope that Coach Jones had handed her. "A gift card to Pizza Moon? This is awesome!" she said. "Thanks so much!"

"You earned it," Coach said, smiling. "See you all at practice tomorrow."

Smiling, Becca walked off the field and headed for her bike, which she'd locked to the fence. But as she carefully opened the lock, she had the strange feeling that she was being watched.

CHAPTER 6
NERVOUS

Becca felt nervous before Friday's practice. She always felt nervous on the day before the first game of the season. But this time was different. She couldn't stop worrying. What if the equipment bag was missing again?

Everyone was gathered around the storage shed when Becca arrived at the field. Her stomach dropped. *Not again*, she thought.

When she noticed Eva running toward the field, carrying two bats and two balls, she knew that her worries were right. Someone had taken the equipment bag again.

"What's going on?" Becca asked Coach Jones.

Coach crossed her arms. "Well, the bag's gone," she said sadly. "Including all the new equipment I bought. Luckily, Eva went home to grab some of her own equipment again."

Coach sighed. Then she said, "I think I'll have to start storing everything at my house. Or buy a lock for the shed."

"Don't you think the person will return the equipment again?" Becca asked hopefully. "Like last time?"

Coach shook her head slowly. "No, I don't," she replied. "Maybe the person felt guilty last time and returned it, but I don't think it'll happen again. Now, let's just move on. Warm up. Then we'll practice hitting."

"But . . ." Becca began.

"No buts," Coach Jones said. "Let's go. We have a game to get ready for."

Becca frowned, but she did what her coach said. She quickly tossed her glove toward the shed. Then she started running laps around the diamond with Eva.

"Can you believe the bag is gone again?" Eva asked.

"I know," Becca said. "It's sort of scary. But I have this weird feeling that the person will bring the bag back again."

Eva shook her head. "I don't think so," she said. "I think Coach is right. Whoever took the bag felt guilty the first time. That's why they brought it back. But then they decided they really did want our stuff. The person must be really mean to steal a softball team's equipment."

"Especially before a game," Becca said sadly. "Good thing you had stuff at your house."

"I know!" Eva replied. "What if I'd left it in the storage shed?"

After warm-ups, the team practiced hitting. That was always one of Becca's favorite things. As she waited for her turn to bat, Becca thought she saw the unfamiliar blond girl hanging around by the fence, but she didn't have time to look more closely.

After she was done batting, Becca looked again, but the strange girl was gone.

As they stood in line to hit again, Becca whispered, "Eva, I think we should have another stakeout tonight."

"Why?" asked Eva. "We fell asleep during the last one, and we didn't catch the thief. Maybe we could do it tomorrow."

"No, I think we have to do it tonight," said Becca. "I have an idea about the bag. Do you think your brother would set the tent up for us again?"

Eva frowned. But before she could say anything, Coach Jones blew her whistle. "Let's go!" Coach called.

"I'll explain after practice," Becca told her friend as quietly as she could. "I promise. I'll come over around eight."

CHAPTER 7
SECOND STAKEOUT

After practice, Becca rode her bike home. Then she ran down the hall to her room. She quickly threw some clean clothes and her softball uniform into a bag.

"What's wrong, Becca?" asked her mom, sounding worried.

"Nothing's wrong," said Becca. "I'm just in a hurry. Can I sleep over at Eva's again tonight? I think I figured out what's going on with our equipment."

Her mom raised her eyebrows. "Sure," she said. "It's after dark now. Why don't I give you a ride to Eva's?"

"Thanks!" said Becca. She hadn't been looking forward to the bike ride in the dark.

When they pulled up in front of Eva's house, the tent was already set up outside.

Becca started to get out of the car. "See you later," she said. She waved as her mother drove away.

After she tossed her bag into the tent, Becca walked across the lawn. But as she stepped onto the sidewalk, she heard a strange noise.

It sounded like it was coming from the softball field across the street. In fact, it sounded like it was coming from the equipment shed!

"Eva!" Becca yelled. "Eva, come outside!"

Eva opened the door. "What is going on?" she asked.

"Someone's in the shed!" whispered Becca.

"Right now?" asked Eva.

Becca nodded. "We have to go check it out," she said. She paused, and then added, "I think I know who it is."

"I don't think it's safe for us to go over there, Becca," Eva said.

"It is," said Becca. "You'll see."

They tiptoed over the lawn and across the street. When they reached the shed, Becca took a deep breath. Then she threw open the door.

CHAPTER 8
HALEY

The blond girl inside the shed dropped the equipment bag and screamed. Balls and bats rolled loudly all over the floor. Eva held on to the flashlight, but she screamed too.

After the screaming ended, the silence in the shed felt heavy. Finally, Becca spoke. "Hi," she said. "My name is Becca." Then she pointed to Eva and said, "This is my friend Eva."

The blond girl had big brown eyes and a friendly face. She smiled nervously. "Um, hi," she said. "My name is Haley, and my family just moved to town. I played softball at my old school, but I didn't know anyone here and my stuff is still in a box, so I've just been borrowing yours so I could practice because I really love softball and I really miss playing."

Becca let out a big breath. Eva bent down to pick up the softballs that had rolled away when Haley dropped the bag.

Haley took a deep breath and looked at Becca and Eva. Becca could see that there were tears in her eyes.

"I just wanted to play softball, but I'm so shy. And you're all such good players," Haley added in a shaky voice.

Then Haley whispered, "Are you going to call the police?"

As calmly as she could, Becca said, "We're not calling the police. But we should get back to Eva's house in case her parents heard all that screaming." Eva and Haley giggled.

Eva pointed and said, "My house is just across the street. Come with us and tell us everything."

The girls headed back across the street. Inside Eva's house, they sat at the kitchen table. Haley told them her story.

"After I finished the school year," she began, "my parents moved us here. We actually live on the other side of the field from you, Eva."

"Cool!" Eva said. "We're neighbors!"

Haley went on, "It was too late to register and try out, but I still really wanted to play. I've been borrowing and returning the bag so I could practice with my brother. I didn't mean to cause any trouble."

Becca decided she liked Haley. Haley hadn't been trying to wreck the team's chances after all. She'd just wanted to play softball.

Then Eva smiled and asked, "Do you think your parents would let you spend the night here in the tent with Becca and me?"

"Really?" Haley asked. "You want me to spend the night? You're not mad?"

"Mad?" asked Becca. "Not at all! We could really use you on the team! I mean, Coach Jones will probably want you to try out, but I'm sure you'll make it."

Haley looked like she couldn't believe her ears. Eva added, "It's not like you kept the equipment. We didn't end up missing practice or anything."

Then Becca said, "And we have a game here tomorrow. I bet you could help Coach with stats and stuff until you can try out on Monday."

Haley looked down at her shoes. Her hair fell in her face. "I hope," she said quietly. "I hope your coach will understand."

CHAPTER 9
CONFESSION

The next morning, Eva's mom unzipped the tent's entrance. "Wake up!" she said.

"What time is it?" groaned Eva.

"It's eight thirty," said Eva's mom. "But I ran into Coach Jones at the grocery store. I told her about Haley, and she wants her to try out this morning so she can play in the game this afternoon."

"What?" said Haley, sitting up in her sleeping bag.

All three girls were wide awake.

"Yes," said Eva's mom. "Ashley's family is on vacation, so that leaves nine players."

"But nine is enough to play," Haley said.

Eva's mom smiled. "It's enough to play, but Coach Jones said that she'll need someone to help her and to play if someone gets hurt," she explained. "Come on, get up. You'll eat breakfast and then you can run home to change, Haley. You need to meet Coach on the field at 11 o'clock sharp!"

* * *

After breakfast, Haley headed home to change her clothes. Eva and Becca changed into their softball uniforms. They sat together on the porch, waiting for their new friend to come back.

"Poor Haley," said Eva. "It would be so hard to move and leave all of your friends and not be able to play softball! I hope Coach lets her play with us today."

"Me too," said Becca.

They were silent for a few moments. Then Eva asked, "How did you know she was the one borrowing the bag?"

"Well, I kept seeing her every day while we were at practice," said Becca. "She was always watching us, but no one seemed to recognize her. And when the bag came back and you said it seemed like someone was borrowing it, I just started thinking."

In a few minutes, Haley was back. The three girls headed over to the field. They arrived at the dugout at the same time that Coach Jones walked up.

"You must be Haley," Coach Jones said.

Haley smiled nervously and took a deep breath. "I am," she said. "But before you let me try out, I need to tell you something." She looked at Becca. Becca nodded at her.

"What is it?" Coach Jones asked.

Haley took another deep breath. "Well," she began, "I'm the one who took the equipment bag."

Coach Jones looked shocked. "What do you mean?" she asked.

Haley looked at the ground. "I never meant to keep it," she said. "I only wanted to borrow it. And two times, I wasn't able to get it back here in time before you started practice. I'm really sorry."

Coach frowned. "I'm really sorry to hear that," she said. "Why did you do it?"

Haley quickly answered, "I just wanted to practice. I moved here too late to sign up for softball, and I knew I had to keep practicing if I wanted to be on the team during the school year. I never meant to destroy practice for the team. I'm so sorry."

Coach was quiet. After what felt like forever, she gave Haley a small smile.

"All right, Haley," she said. "If you impress me in your tryout, you can be on the team. You'll have to sit out the first two games and just help me. What do you think?"

Haley's eyes grew wide. "Do you mean it?" she whispered. "You'll let me be on the team even though I screwed up?"

Coach laughed. "Yes, Haley," she said. "Now, let's see how you play!"

CHAPTER 10
THAT'S WHAT FRIENDS ARE FOR!

The first thing Coach had Haley do was run around the bases. Haley ran as fast as she could while Coach timed her and Eva and Becca cheered. Becca was surprised to see how fast Haley was, even though she was shorter than Eva.

After Haley was done running, Coach Jones said, "That was great. Now I'm going to have Becca pitch to you and see how hitting goes. Eva, you can catch."

Haley grabbed a bat. She took a few practice swings before she stepped up to the plate. Becca wasn't really a pitcher, but she knew how to do it. She wound up and fired the ball toward Eva's glove.

Haley swung hard. The bat made a loud clang. The ball sailed into the outfield between first and second base. If they had been playing, Haley would have easily had a base hit.

Becca threw a few more pitches. Then Coach Jones gave them a few minutes to get drinks of water.

Becca asked Haley, "Why were you scared that you wouldn't make the team? You're awesome!"

Haley blushed and smiled. "Thanks," she said. "I hope she lets me on the team."

"Are you kidding?" asked Eva. "Of course she will!"

Haley's tryout went on for about twenty more minutes. Finally, Coach Jones smiled and said, "Well, I've seen enough. You're on the team."

Haley grinned from ear to ear. "Thank you, Coach!" she said happily. "I promise you won't regret it."

"Great," said Coach Jones. "Why don't you guys go have some lunch before the game starts? I'll see you back here in a little while."

After the coach walked away, Haley said, "Thanks a lot, you guys. That was awesome. I feel great!"

"Hey, no problem," Becca said. "After all, that's what friends are for."

Haley laughed. "You know, my mom kept saying I shouldn't worry, that I'd make friends. I guess I could have picked an easier way to make them!"

Eva and Becca laughed. "Come on," Eva said. "Let's get some lunch. We have a game to win this afternoon!"

Arm in arm, the three friends walked across the street to Eva's house.

ABOUT THE AUTHOR

Val Priebe lives in Minneapolis with her two miniature dachshunds, Bruce and Lily. The last time she played softball, she hit her sister in the leg with a line drive to second base. She thinks her sister has forgiven her. Val works at a law firm, but in her free time she coaches basketball and writes books like this one.

ABOUT THE ILLUSTRATOR

When Tuesday Mourning was a little girl, she knew she wanted to be an artist when she grew up. Now, she is an illustrator who lives in Knoxville, Tennessee. She especially loves illustrating books for kids and teenagers. When she isn't illustrating, Tuesday loves spending time with her husband, who is an actor, and their son, Atticus.

GLOSSARY

crew (KROO)—a team of people who work together

dugout (DUHG-out)—a shelter where softball or baseball players sit when they are not at bat or in the field

equipment (i-KWIP-muhnt)—the tools needed to play a particular sport

fielder (FEEL-dur)—a player who has a position in the outfield

league (LEEG)—a group of sports teams

negative (NEG-uh-tiv)—a negative number is less than zero

recognize (REK-uhg-nize)—see someone and know who they are

required (ree-KWI-urd)—if you are required to do something, you must do it

shortstop (SHORT-stop)—the player whose position is between second and third base

thief (THEEF)—someone who steals

unfamiliar (uhn-fuh-MIL-yur)—not known

THE ABCs OF SOFTBALL

At Bats is how many times a player has hit in a game

Bullpen is where a relief pitcher warms up

Catcher is the player who sits behind home plate and catches the pitches

Diamond is the shape made by all four bases

Error is a mistake made by a player in the field that lets a runner advance

Fly Ball is when a batter hits the ball high and straight up in the air

Ground Ball is a ball that is hit so that it rolls or bounces on the ground

Home Run is when a ball is hit over the fence and the batter touches all the bases safely to score a run

Inning is each turn a team gets to both bat and play defense

Line Drive is when a ball is hit in the air but not very high

Outfield is the grassy area beyond the bases

Pitcher is the player who throws balls for the batters to swing at

Run is a point scored when a player safely crosses home plate

Safe means that a runner has made it to a base before the ball

Triple is a hit that allows the batter to run all the way to third base safely

Walk is when the pitcher throws four pitches that are outside of the batter's strike zone. Then the batter gets to go to first base without hitting the ball.

DISCUSSION QUESTIONS

1. Why did Haley borrow the equipment bag? What other options did she have if she wanted to play softball?

2. On page 6, Eva said that she wished there were some new girls on the team. Why do you think she felt that way?

3. Did Eva and Becca do the right thing when they looked in the storage shed to find the thief? Why or why not?

WRITING PROMPTS

1. Imagine that you're Haley. Write a letter to a friend in your old town. Tell your friend about your new softball team and about how your summer is going.

2. During the summer, Eva and Becca play softball. What's your favorite summer activity? Write about it.

3. This book could have had a different ending. What if Becca and Eva opened the shed door and someone else (not Haley) was inside? Write a new ending to the book, starting with Becca and Eva finding someone else in the storage shed.

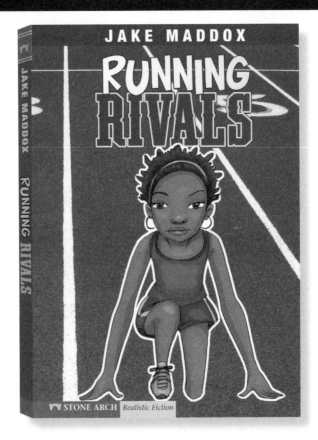

Amy hurt her knee during a race. Her knee may be healed, but her confidence is still broken. The biggest race of the year is coming up, and it's on the exact same track where she was hurt before. With help from an unexpected source, will she be able to race again?

BY JAKE MADDOX

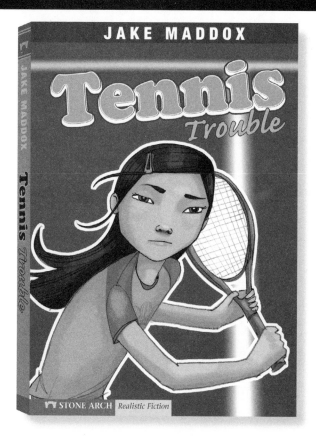

Alexis made the varsity tennis team, but not everyone is happy for her. Some older girls are out to make Alexis's season terrible. Can she keep up her self-confidence and step up to the net, or will she let the girls get to her and lose everything?

INTERNET SITES

Do you want to know more about subjects related to this book? Or are you interested in learning about other topics? Then check out FactHound, a fun, easy way to find Internet sites.

Our investigative staff has already sniffed out great sites for you!

Here's how to use FactHound:

1. Visit *www.facthound.com*

2. Select your grade level.

3. To learn more about subjects related to this book, type in the book's ISBN number: **9781434207791**.

4. Click the **Fetch It** button.

FactHound will fetch the best Internet sites for you!